HOW TO BE A NINJA

Written by Rosie Peet

Editor Rosie Peet
Designer James McKeag
Pre-production Producer Siu Yin Chan
Producer Lloyd Robertson
Managing Editor Paula Regan
Design Manager Jo Connor
Publisher Julie Ferris
Art Director Lisa Lanzarini
Publishing Director Simon Beecroft

First American Edition, 2020
Published in the United States by DK Publishing
1450 Broadway, Suite 801, New York,
New York 10018

Page design copyright © 2020 Dorling Kindersley Limited
DK, a Division of Penguin Random House LLC
20 21 22 23 24 10 9 8 7 6 5 4 3 2 1
001–316424–Jan/2020

A catalog record for this book is available from the Library of Congress.

ISBN: 978-1-4654-8994-4 (Paperback)
ISBN: 978-1-4654-9047-6 (Hardback)

DK books are available at special discounts when purchased in bulk for sales promotions, premiums,
fund-raising, or educational use. For details, contact: DK Publishing SpecialMarkets, 1450 Broadway,
Suite 801, New York, New York 10018
SpecialSales@dk.com

Printed and bound in China

A WORLD OF IDEAS:
SEE ALL THERE IS TO KNOW

www.dk.com
www.LEGO.com

Contents

3

Ninja training

In the land of Ninjago live six ninja. These brave warriors keep the land safe. Their names are Nya, Jay, Cole, Lloyd, Kai, and Zane.

Jay

Master Wu

Nya

The ninja's teacher is Master Wu. He trains the ninja to be skilled fighters. He doesn't like laziness!

Cole

Kai

Lloyd

Zane

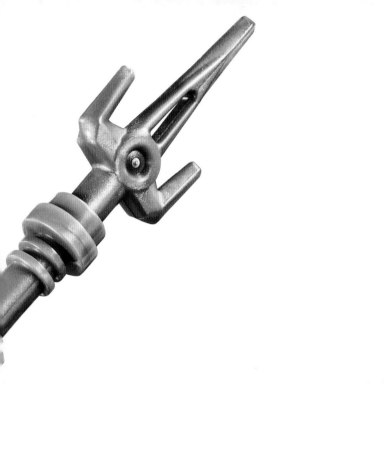

The ninja train hard. They learn how to use cool weapons.

Nya is learning how to use a trident. It has three prongs. It has a dragon on the handle.

The ninja also train in the art of Spinjitzu. They spin really fast to create a tornado of energy. These tornados make them powerful in their battles.

Cole is practicing Spinjitzu. He has created a tornado of fire!

Master Wu has set up a training challenge for Lloyd. Lloyd must use Spinjitzu to grab a sword from a high platform.

Lloyd must be careful. If he lands on the wrong platform, he will meet a creepy spider!

A ninja must be agile as well as fast. Master Wu has created an obstacle course to train Jay.

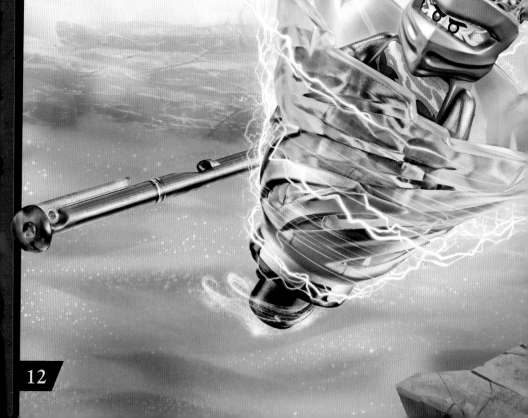

Jay must dodge the flying missiles. It is hard to avoid missiles when you are spinning so fast!

It is time for Zane's training! He must hit the target on the training dummy. He also needs to avoid some flying blades. Zane uses Spinjitzu to dodge the blades and reach the dummy.

Kai puts his training into action! He wants to grab a sword. It is a powerful weapon. He jumps and spins toward it.

An enemy Blizzard Warrior has the same idea! Who will get there first?

Desert duels

The ninja chase enemies in their
vehicles. Ninja must be able to
travel on land, on water, and in
the air.

Master Wu steers his flyer over the hot desert. Nya follows in a speedy quad bike.

Wu's flyer and Nya's quad bike fit onto the Land Bounty. The Land Bounty is the ninja's main vehicle. It has sails like a ship. It has six wheels. It can drive over rocky ground.

Main sail

©2019 The LEGO Group

Master Wu's flyer

Side cannon

2508   LAND BOUNTY

Chunky wheels

Cole and Nya are battling under the hot sun. They are fighting the sneaky snakes. Nya uses her Spinjitzu skills to attack Char. Cole rides in on his Dirt Bike to face Pyro Whipper.

Aspheera is a Serpentine with magical powers. She is a fierce enemy. She rides a giant snake called Fire Fang across the desert. Fire Fang has sharp fangs and can breathe fire!

Nya has come face to face
with Aspheera and Fire Fang.
Watch out, Nya! Fire Fang
has fiery breath and a
thrashing tail!

Thrashing tail

Swords

Aspheera's throne

Fiery breath

The Never-Realm

Zane is flying his Shuricopter over the icy Never-Realm. He is looking for the Scroll of Forbidden Spinjitzu.

The Shuricopter has two sets of sharp blades at the front. It shoots missiles from two cannons.

Jay is battling an Ice Warrior. The Ice Warrior has the scroll on a long sword.

Jay uses his Spinjitzu skills to try to grab the scroll. The Ice Warrior dodges out of the way.

Lloyd is battling a fierce Blizzard Warrior. Lloyd remembers his training. He puts his sword skills into action!

Lloyd's friend Akita can turn into a wolf with three tails. She sneaks up on the icy foe. Lloyd and Akita defeat the Blizzard Warrior together.

Zane and Lloyd are taking on a whole army of Blizzard Warriors! Zane uses his Spinjitzu powers against two enemies. A Blizzard Archer and a Blizzard Sword Master are no match for Lloyd's mighty Titan Mech.

The ninja see something in the sky. It is the Forbidden Ice Dragon! This dragon has huge wings, sharp claws, and a long tail.

The Forsaken Emperor sits on the Dragon's back. He is holding the scroll!

Lloyd, Cole, and Akita
follow the dragon to the
Castle of the Forsaken
Emperor. Blizzard Warriors
fire arrows from tall towers.

The Forsaken Emperor sits
on a high throne. Lloyd tries
to reach him but he gets
trapped in icicles! Lloyd uses
Spinjitzu to break free.

The Emperor has come down from his throne. Lloyd battles against him one-on-one! Lloyd puts his Spinjitzu training into practice.

Lloyd spins fast and dodges the
Emperor's blade. Lloyd is so fast
that he is able to grab the scroll
from the Emperor!

The ninja drive cool vehicles, use awesome weapons, and spin like tornados. They use their skills to defeat fierce enemies.

The ninja are ready to face anything. Master Wu is proud of his students. Now you know how to be a ninja, too!

Quiz

1. Who is the ninja's teacher?

2. Which power lets the ninja spin like tornados?

3. What is the name of the ninja's main vehicle?

4. Which ninja has a Dirt Bike?

5. What is the name of Aspheera's giant snake?

6. True or false? Akita can turn into a polar bear with three tails.

7. What kind of flying animal does the Emperor ride?

8. What does Lloyd get stuck in at the Castle of the Forsaken Emperor?

Answers on page 47

Glossary

foe
Enemy

forsaken
Abandoned or left alone.

obstacle course
A series of challenges to test someone's strength and agility.

quad bike
A motorbike with four wheels.

tornado
Strong winds that whirl in a spiral.

trident
A type of weapon that has three prongs.

warrior
Someone who fights in battles.

Index

Answers to the quiz on pages 44 and 45:
1. Master Wu 2. Spinjitzu 3. The Land Bounty 4. Cole
5. Fire Fang 6. False. She can turn into a wolf with three tails.
7. A dragon 8. Icicles

A LEVEL FOR EVERY READER

This book is a part of an exciting four-level reading series to support children in developing the habit of reading widely for both pleasure and information. Each book is designed to develop a child's reading skills, fluency, grammar awareness, and comprehension in order to build confidence and enjoyment when reading.

Ready for a Level 2 (Beginning to Read) book

A child should:

- be able to recognize a bank of common words quickly and be able to blend sounds together to make some words.
- be familiar with using beginner letter sounds and context clues to figure out unfamiliar words.
- sometimes correct his/her reading if it doesn't look right or make sense.
- be aware of the need for a slight pause at commas and a longer one at periods.

A valuable and shared reading experience

For many children, reading requires much effort, but adult participation can make reading both fun and easier. Here are a few tips on how to use this book with a young reader:

Check out the contents together:

- read about the book on the back cover and talk about the contents page to help heighten interest and expectation.
- discuss new or difficult words.
- chat about labels, annotations, and pictures.

Support the reader:

- give the book to the young reader to turn the pages.
- where necessary, encourage longer words to be broken into syllables, sound out each one, and then flow the syllables together; ask him/her to reread the sentence to check the meaning.
- encourage the reader to vary her/his voice as she/he reads; demonstrate how to do this if helpful.

Talk at the end of each page:

- ask questions about the text and the meaning of some of the words used—this helps develop comprehension skills.
- read the quiz at the end of the book and encourage the reader to answer the questions, if necessary, by turning back to the relevant pages to find the answers.